MW00887761

# MY SKIN, YOUR SKIN. WHERE DO GENES BEGIN?

A children's book about siblings who have the same parents but different skin complexions.

"Zoom! Zoom! You can't catch me!" Devon said as he raced his toy car past Aria's.

"Wait for me!" Aria shouted, pushing her own car forward.

Devon slowed down to let his little sister catch up. As she raced to the finish line, his curious eye caught onto her tan hand.

Devon looked down at his own brown hand resting by his side. He had never thought about it before, but his hand and Aria's weren't the same color.

"I win! I win!" Aria shouted, dancing around.

But Devon barely heard her. Suddenly, the color of his hand seemed more important than the toy car race.

"Why do Aria and I look different?" he asked his parents. "We both have the same Mommy and Daddy, but her skin is so much lighter than mine."
Aria sank to the floor next to her brother. "Yeah, why is my skin lighter?" she asked, copying Devon like usual.

"Well, it has a lot to do with genes," Dad said. "What are genes, Mommy?!" Aria yelled.

Devon looked at his shorts. "Like the jeans we put on?" he asked.

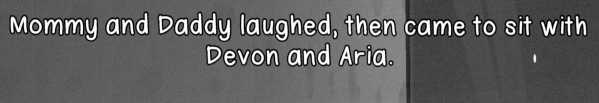

Mommy and Daddy laughed, then came to sit with Devon and Aria.

Mommy pulled Aria onto her lap. "Genes are what God uses to give everyone their features, from how tall someone is, to the color of their eyes."

"Mommy and I have different genes. When we had you, they came together to create your features," Daddy explained.

"So do Aria and I have different genes?" Devon asked.

"You do," Daddy said. "But you also have some that are the same because your genes are both from the same place, me and Mommy. That's what makes you brother and sister, even if you do look a little different."

"Devon," Mommy said, "you get your brown skin and eyebrows from me, and your hair and ears from Daddy."

"And Aria gets her light skin and eyes from me, and her ears and curly hair from Mommy," Daddy said.

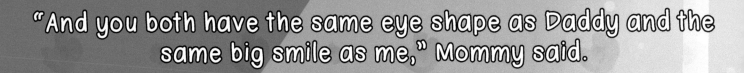

"And you both have the same eye shape as Daddy and the same big smile as me," Mommy said.

"So that means no matter what color our skin is, we both share the same genes?" Devon asked.

"That's right," Daddy said. "Your genes come from Mommy and me, and no matter how they make you look, we are all one family."

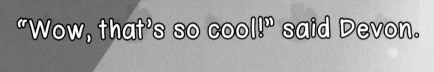

"Wow, that's so cool!" said Devon.

"Yeah, so cool," Aria said with a bright smile that looked the same as her brother's.

Feeling better, Devon and Aria returned to their race. Suddenly, Aria looked up from her car and said, "I know something about us that is all the same. We're best friends and we love each other!"

"You're right. We are best friends, and I love you so much," Devon said, hugging Aria.

As Devon went back to playing with his cars, he smiled. He knew now that no matter what color his skin was, he loves the skin he has, because every shade was beautiful, and every shade was part of his family!

CPSIA information can be obtained
at www.ICGtesting.com
Printed in the USA
BVHW020728120421
604722BV00012B/128

9 781736 765302